The Rescue Princesses

The Stolen Crystals

More amazing animal adventures!

The Secret Promise

The Wishing Pearl

The Moonlight Mystery

The Rescue Princesses

The Stolen Crystals

♥ **PAULA HARRISON** ♥

Scholastic Inc.

For Mum and Dad, with much love

ISBN 978-0-545-50916-9

Text copyright © 2012 by Paula Harrison
Interior illustrations copyright © 2012 by Artful Doodlers

All rights reserved. Published by Scholastic Inc., 557 Broadway, New York, NY 10012, by arrangement with Nosy Crow Ltd.

12 11 10   16 17 18/0

Printed in the U.S.A.   40

First printing, August 2013

CHAPTER ONE

The Master Gem Maker

Princess Jaminta dashed up the stairs with her long green cloak flying out behind her. She ran into her bedroom, undid her cloak, and threw it onto the bed. Her brown eyes sparkled.

She'd just gone to see the little panda cub that lived on Cloud Mountain with his mother. He was a sweet thing, with big black eyes and a cuddly white tummy. She wished she could have stayed up there all day.

Quickly, she gave herself a shake. She had to stop daydreaming about the little cub! She had something important to do.

She hurried to her dressing table and picked up a small lump of white rock that lay in front of the mirror. It was time to do something special with this crystal rock.

She had made it by sticking lots of tiny crystals together. It didn't look very pretty yet. But once she had worked on it with her jewel-making tools, it would turn into a beautiful gem that would be perfect for her grandfather's birthday present. She had to hurry, though. His birthday was tomorrow, and soon the other royal families from all over the world would be arriving to help them celebrate.

She unfolded her pouch of jewel-making tools and picked up a silver chisel. Her smooth, dark hair curled around her chin as she leaned forward. Holding the rock crystal still, she tapped on the chisel with a tiny hammer. She was planning to smooth its sides and change its shape.

Maybe she'd make it heart-shaped, just like the famous Onica Heart Crystals that used to belong to her grandfather. Those Heart Crystals had vanished a long time ago, but everyone in the kingdom still talked about them.

She tapped the rock harder. Delicate white flakes chipped off and dropped onto the dressing table. But the crystal still looked rough and absolutely refused to sparkle.

Jaminta frowned. Why was it so difficult? It wasn't as if she'd never done this before. She'd been making jewels for years. She'd even made the special rings that she and the other Rescue Princesses used to call one another when they needed help. She smiled for a moment, thinking of Emily, Clarabel, and Lulu. Together, they had made a secret promise always to help an animal in trouble. She was so proud that her special jewels played an important part in their animal rescues.

She gripped the chisel tightly, and swiftly tapped the rock crystal again with her hammer. There was a snap, and a jagged crack ran all the way down the side of the rock. Jaminta gasped. She'd tapped too hard. How could she have been so careless?

She should have started making the jewel weeks ago instead of spending all her time with the panda cub. Now it was too late to make Grandfather a different present. She rubbed her eyes with the back of her hand. The jewel was ruined. Unless . . . maybe . . . She'd nearly forgotten about the one person who could help.

She flung the tools down and fled from the room, taking the lump of rock with her. Swift as a mountain deer, she ran down five flights of stairs. She passed the kitchens, where the clash of saucepans told her that the banquet was cooking.

She passed the great hall, where her mother was layering twelve round tiers of birthday cake on top of one another. In the driveway, she passed the servants hanging red and gold paper lanterns between every tree.

Ignoring all the party preparations, Jaminta hurried down the outside steps and along a winding path. She stopped in front of a wooden hut in the farthest corner of the garden. The sound of clinking metal came from inside, and a warm orange light shone from the windows. This was where the Master Gem Maker worked, and he knew more about crafting jewels than anyone else in the kingdom of Onica.

Jaminta knocked on the door.

A small man with half-moon glasses opened the door and bowed. "Good afternoon, Princess Jaminta. Aren't you getting ready for the party? I thought all the royal visitors were arriving today." He stepped aside to let Jaminta through the door.

"They should be here very soon," said Jaminta. "But I was just trying to finish Grandfather's present, and then something went wrong." She held out the lump of crystal for him to see. The crack running down one side seemed even bigger than before.

The Master Gem Maker took the rough jewel from her hand and studied it carefully with a magnifying glass.

Jaminta watched him anxiously. Then she swept a quick look around the room. The workshop was crammed with even more jewels and equipment than the last time she had been here. Shelves lined the walls, full of tools and little pots of polish.

A wooden chest stood open on the floor, bursting with every kind of gem. There were ocean-blue sapphires, forest-green emeralds, and rubies as red as fire. They dazzled her eyes and sent sparkles of colored light dancing across the wooden ceiling. She remembered how she used to come here every day when she was little to learn jewel crafting from the Master.

"What kind of gem are you trying to make?" asked the Master Gem Maker.

"I wanted to make it heart-shaped because it's for Grandfather's birthday," Jaminta said miserably. "He always says that the kingdom hasn't been the same since the Onica Heart Crystals were stolen. I thought if I made him a crystal that looked the same, he'd be pleased."

"It's been nearly ten years since the Heart Crystals were stolen," said the Master. "Each one was as clear as a diamond, with a flickering flame right in the center. Those jewels were so magical that they could reveal the true nature of a person's heart."

A gust of wind from the mountains swept around the hut, sending an icy chill under the door and making the windows rattle.

Jaminta bit her lip. "I collected lots of tiny crystals at a place called Shimmer Rock and stuck them all together. I thought it would be beautiful."

The Master placed the rock crystal back into Jaminta's hand and looked at her over the top of his spectacles. "You can still make something special. You just need to do one more thing."

Jaminta felt her heart leap. "What is it? What do I have to do?"

"You must dip it into the Silver River."

Jaminta stared at him, openmouthed. "Really? I just have to put it in the river?"

The Master Gem Maker smiled. "The river has a natural magic. You can't use it to turn a frog into a prince or a pumpkin into a carriage, but you can make a crystal its true shape. Go there at sunrise. That's when the magic is strongest."

"I'll go first thing tomorrow." Jaminta's face glowed. She could just imagine how beautiful the jewel was going to look and how happy her grandfather would be when she gave it to him.

The Master smiled. "Remember! Only tell people that you really trust about your crystal. They're very precious things!"

"I'll remember," said Jaminta. "Thank you!" She hid the rock in her pocket and opened the door, then turned back for a moment. "If only I could find the lost Onica Heart Crystals for Grandfather as well!"

The Master Gem Maker's eyes turned hazy, as if he was gazing at something far away. "Crystals are full of surprises. Maybe one day the Heart Crystals will return."

Jaminta was about to ask him what he meant, but just then the deep, clear sound of a bell rang out from the palace.

Jaminta caught her breath. That was the signal. The royal visitors were arriving. Soon she would see the other Rescue Princesses again!

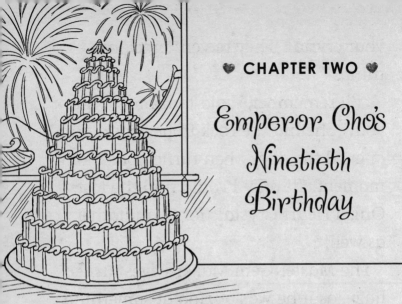

CHAPTER TWO

Emperor Cho's Ninetieth Birthday

Jaminta raced back toward the palace, a fizzing feeling growing inside her. She could hardly believe that the river was magical, although she'd always thought it was special somehow. Now she knew exactly how to turn her rock crystal into a finished jewel in time for Grandfather's birthday.

Her grandfather was Emperor Cho, the ruler of the kingdom of Onica, and tomorrow he would be ninety years old.

There would be games, feasting, and fireworks. Jaminta could hardly wait! More than anything, she longed to show the Rescue Princesses her beautiful panda cub. She knew they would love him as much as she did.

The bell rang out again from the top of the high pagoda roof.

Jaminta scanned the driveway, but there was no sign of the visitors yet. She ran up the palace steps and gazed at the purple mountain peaks soaring beyond the river. Thick green bamboo forests stretched halfway up the slopes, leaving bare rock at the very top. The cold breeze from the mountains tickled her cheeks. It wasn't winter yet, but soon the peaks would be covered in snow.

She swung around as her grandfather came out of the palace door behind her.

"There you are, Jaminta!" Emperor

Cho climbed slowly down the steps. His gray hair looked thin, but his brown eyes twinkled at her.

Jaminta smiled back, secretly checking that her rock crystal was hidden deep inside her pocket. Tomorrow at sunrise she would take it down to the river, just like the Master Gem Maker had told her.

"Are the visitors almost here, Grandfather?" she asked.

"Yes. Look, you can see the carriages." The emperor pointed at the road that led up from the valley.

Jaminta spotted the long caterpillar of carriages trundling up the hill. As they moved closer, she could see kings, queens, princes, and princesses waving from the carriage windows. Her eyes searched for three princesses, one with black hair, one with golden hair, and one with wild red curls.

Soon the carriages climbed the hill to the palace gate and passed between stone pillars topped with statues of dragons. They came to a stop. Princess Emily appeared, climbing out of the first carriage, her red curls waving in the breeze.

"Emily!" Jaminta hugged her friend. "I'm so happy you could come!"

"Hello, Jaminta!" said Emily, hugging her back.

Emily's parents, the king and queen of Middingland, climbed out next. Then Emily's maid, Ally, appeared carrying Emily's pink suitcase. She smiled at Jaminta, who grinned back. Ally had once been an undercover agent who caught jewel thieves. She had used ninja skills when she was an agent and taught them to the princesses to help with their animal rescues.

"Your Majesties!" Emperor Cho bowed to the king and queen of Middingland. "Thank you for coming all this way to celebrate my birthday!"

Suddenly, another figure hopped out of the Middingland carriage. She looked just like Emily, except that her red hair was even curlier and her eyes were a sparkling green.

"Hurry *up*, Lottie. You're being so slow." Emily turned to Jaminta. "This is my little sister, Lottie. She didn't come along the last time the royal families gathered together because she was staying with our cousins."

"Hello, Lottie." Jaminta smiled.

Lottie stuck out her tongue and then grinned.

The next carriage came to a halt, and a tall man with a red cloak and a crooked mouth climbed out, followed by his servant.

"Welcome back to Onica, Earl Scrant," said the emperor. "I don't think we've met for many years."

"Greetings." Earl Scrant bowed stiffly before walking away. Unluckily, he bumped right into Ally and sent the pink suitcase flying. He glared at her and then marched away, his red cloak billowing out around him.

"Sorry, sir. Please excuse me," said Ally, darting a mysterious look at the earl.

Jaminta noticed Ally's strange glance as she ran over to help pick up the suitcase.

One by one, Emperor Cho greeted all the other royal guests. Jaminta's mom and dad, the king and queen of Onica, came to greet the visitors, too. The orchestra played a beautiful tune, and trays of honey cakes were brought around for everyone.

Emperor Cho clapped his hands. "Ladies and gentlemen, kings and queens," he announced, "welcome to the kingdom of Onica. There will be feasting, fireworks, and a twelve-tier birthday cake! This has always been a land of adventures and we hope you enjoy your stay very much!"

A buzz of excitement came from a group of princes standing nearby. "Adventures!" cried Prince George. "I want something really exciting to happen!"

"Poor princes!" said a voice behind Jaminta's ear. "They'll never have the best adventures with us around!"

Jaminta spun around to find Princess Lulu, with her black curls and flashing eyes, standing behind her, grinning. Next to her stood a smiling Princess Clarabel, tucking her golden hair behind her ear.

"Lulu! Clarabel!" cried Jaminta, hugging them both. "I'm so glad you're here! I have something really special I want to show you." She beckoned her three friends to follow her to the palace gate. She would take them right up to Cloud Mountain to see the panda cub and tell them her big secret about Grandfather's birthday present and the magical river on the way.

"Jaminta! Princesses! Come back, please!" the queen of Onica called after them. "You must all come with me and choose a fan for the banquet tonight. It's an important custom here in the kingdom of Onica for ladies to carry fans, you know! It will make you look graceful and elegant." She began to shepherd the princesses toward the palace door.

Jaminta groaned. She wished her mom hadn't noticed them sneaking away.

"Don't worry!" whispered Clarabel, squeezing her hand. "Maybe this won't take long."

"Come along, princesses!" said the queen. "You're very lucky girls to be borrowing Onican fans. Put your best dresses on and then join me in the Fan Room." She waved her hand majestically to send them hurrying away.

Jaminta clomped up the stairs, frowning. Who wanted to spend time looking at fans when there was a cute panda cub to play with?

CHAPTER THREE

Fan-tastic Princesses

Jaminta showed her friends to their rooms, then trudged to her own. She pulled her new dress out of her closet. It had been sewn especially for the emperor's birthday celebration and was made of shimmering green silk decorated with gold blossoms. It had wide sleeves that hung elegantly below her arms. She pulled it over her head and dropped the rock crystal that she'd taken to the Master Gem Maker into her pocket. Then she added a gold tiara, and with one last look in the mirror, she made her way to the Fan Room.

The other princesses arrived in their best dresses, too. Emily was wearing a pink dress with a wide skirt, while Clarabel's dress was very long and pale blue. Lulu, who was gazing longingly out the window at the mountains, wore a shorter yellow dress decorated with beads.

"Ready, girls?" said the queen. "Let me show you our fan collection." She opened a large display case filled with beautiful fans in every color. Many of them glimmered with sequins or tiny pearls. Jaminta chose one that had been painted with a picture of the Silver River and the mountains beyond.

When all the princesses had finished choosing, the queen closed the case again. "Now I'll show you how to use

them. Place your thumb behind the fan, like this." She twisted the fan, showing them what she meant. "Then you must make the fan flutter quickly and delicately, like this."

The princesses copied her, trying hard to use the fan just as elegantly. Lulu flapped hers a bit too hard and knocked off Jaminta's tiara, sending them both into fits of giggles.

A maid appeared in the doorway and curtsied. "Excuse me, Your Majesty. The Chief Cook would like to speak to you about the noodles."

"Keep practicing, girls," said the queen as she hurried away. "Remember, the banquet starts at six o'clock. Don't be late!"

"Yes, Your Majesty," they all said, curtsying.

"I think these fans are lovely," said Clarabel, waving hers, which was decorated with pearls and soft blue feathers.

Lulu groaned. "They're nice, but I want to stop waving them now. I mean, what good are they?"

"I know!" said Emily suddenly, her hazel eyes sparkling. "They could be really handy for our ninja moves!"

"Really?" said Lulu. "How would you use a fan for ninja moves?"

Emily flipped her fan open in front of her face, disappearing behind its red-and-gold pattern. "See? You can hide behind them!"

"You can do more than that," said Jaminta. "I've been using them since I was little. Watch this!" She flicked her wrist, sending her fan across the room in a graceful arc. It swept over the top of a fruit bowl, knocking into a bunch of oranges, which rolled away across the floor. The fan landed on the windowsill and closed with a neat snap.

"Awesome!" said Lulu. "You have to teach us how to do that!"

"Are you sure we're allowed to use them like that?" asked Clarabel, her blue eyes wide.

"Don't worry! The fans are too strong to get damaged," said Jaminta. "It's really easy. I'll show you!" She retrieved her fan and flicked it again, making it land in exactly the same place on the windowsill.

The other princesses each took their turns, and soon there was a flurry of whizzing fans and falling oranges.

"I'll tell Ally about this," said Emily. "Maybe she knows some ninja moves using fans as well."

When the fruit bowl was empty, the princesses hurried to gather up the fallen oranges. Some had rolled away under a long table, so they crawled underneath it to collect them. They were just about to crawl out again, when they heard voices and heavy footsteps.

Jaminta pulled the others back under the table and yanked the tablecloth down to hide them. "If we climb out now, we'll get yelled at for not being all prim and proper!" she hissed. "Let's stay under here till they've left."

The voices grew louder. Jaminta peered out from under the fringe of the tablecloth and saw two pairs of men's shoes walk across the room and stop next to the window. The first set of shoes was black and had been polished to a high shine. The other shoes were brown and scuffed.

Jaminta thought she caught a glimpse of red material as they passed by. But she couldn't see much more without sticking her head right out into the open.

"Hurry up!" said a man in a thin, bossy voice. "I have something important to say and I don't want everyone hearing it."

Jaminta's heart raced. What was it that this man didn't want other people to hear?

"We're going up the mountain to look for those lost things," said the thin voice. "Make sure you bring your shovel with you."

"What things, Your Grace?" asked a second man, sounding confused.

"Wake up!" snapped the thin voice. "The special things I left here ten years ago. You know what I'm talking about."

"But, Your Grace! We searched for them several times. You said they were lost."

"We couldn't look for them well enough back then because we were being followed," said the thin voice, rising in annoyance. "But this is a perfect opportunity. It's not often I get to come back to Onica without everyone getting suspicious. Once I've found a likely place, you will begin digging."

A hand closed around Jaminta's wrist. It was Emily. She pointed at the polished black shoes and made a face.

Jaminta wasn't sure what she meant and didn't dare ask out loud. Her mind was whirling. What were the men looking for on the mountainside? And why was it so secret?

CHAPTER FOUR

Gem Song

The princesses tried to keep completely still under the table as the men continued to talk.

"But what if the sun goes down while I'm there on the mountainside?" said the second man. "They say huge black-and-white bears roam the forest."

"They're pandas, you brainless fool! They won't hurt you," said the thin voice. "Now, meet me by the bridge in two hours and don't forget your shovel."

"Yes, My Lord," came the low reply, and the scuffed brown shoes marched away.

The black shoes stayed by the window for a few minutes, then they left, too. The princesses crawled out, carefully checking that the room was empty.

"Whew!" said Clarabel. "I thought they were never going to leave."

"I've met one of them before," said Emily. "That's what I was trying to tell you. I recognize the voice of the bossy one, the one in the black shoes."

"Is he from Middingland?" asked Lulu.

Emily screwed up her face, thinking hard. "Yes, that must be how I know him. I just can't remember his name."

Jaminta put the oranges back in the bowl and picked up her fan. "I wonder what they're looking for. I've never heard of anything being lost on the mountain.

I hope they don't disturb the animals when they go up there."

"Are there really pandas in the forest?" asked Clarabel.

"Yes, there are!" said Jaminta. "We could sneak away and see them, now that my mom's gone to the kitchens." She grinned. "And guess what? One of the pandas is a baby!"

"A baby panda! How lovely!" cried Clarabel, her blue eyes sparkling.

"I've never seen a panda in real life before!" said Emily. "Is the cub really cute?"

Jaminta nodded. "He's adorable!"

Not wanting to wait another second, the princesses put their fans away in a drawer and raced downstairs. People were still unloading suitcases from the carriages and carrying them inside.

Jaminta led them through the gardens. They passed trees with crimson leaves and a pond full of golden fish. At last they reached the back gate to the palace grounds.

Jaminta unfastened the gate. The princesses burst through and raced down the rough, grassy slope. They stopped to catch their breath at the bottom, where a fast-moving river flowed along the valley.

"Oh! I almost forgot! I have something else to show you, too." Jaminta pulled her rock crystal out of her pocket and showed it to them.

The other princesses stared at the lump of rock with its rough edges and dirty white surface.

"Er . . . what is it?" asked Lulu.

"It's a rock crystal," said Jaminta. "I found out the secret of how to change its shape. When I've turned it into a beautiful jewel, I'm going to give it to my grandfather for his birthday."

"So what's the secret? How do you change it?" asked Emily.

"I have to put it in the river at sunrise." Jaminta smiled. "The river will change it, because it's magical."

The princesses stared at the river. It really did look magical with the sunshine dancing on its surface.

"Wow! That's amazing!" said Clarabel. "We'll come with you tomorrow morning to help."

Jaminta smiled gratefully at Clarabel, then Lulu burst out: "That's great, but can we get going now? I'm dying to see the baby panda!"

Jaminta sighed and put the rock back into her pocket. Maybe when the crystal had changed into something beautiful, Lulu would be more interested in it. She wished she could make it happen right now, but the Master Gem Maker had told her that the magic was strongest at sunrise.

The girls walked along to the curved red bridge that arched across the river. Their feet drummed on the wooden planks as they crossed, and the river bubbled over the stones below them. On the other side, the ground sloped steeply upward. They soon found themselves inside a thick forest where bamboo trees stretched straight up to the sky. Now and then they caught a glimpse of the palace below, which became smaller and smaller as they climbed higher up Cloud Mountain.

"I hope those men from the Fan Room aren't around here," said Clarabel nervously.

"Don't worry," said Jaminta. "It's a very big forest, so I'm sure we won't see them."

They pushed their way through the closely growing trees until they reached the edge of a rocky ravine. A narrow rope bridge spanned the steep drop.

"It's best if we go one at a time," Jaminta told them. "The bridge isn't very strong."

One by one, the princesses crossed the swaying rope bridge, trying not to look at the rocks below them. Even Jaminta, who was used to the wobbly bridge, was glad to be safely on the other side.

"There's a clearing up here," she said. "That's where I often see the pandas."

Listening carefully, the girls crept toward a gap in the trees. The sound of cracking and rustling came from up ahead. Jaminta smiled. That would be the mother panda, pulling down bamboo to feed herself and her baby.

A sudden tug on her pocket made her check the rock crystal. It felt heavier somehow. Maybe she was just tired from all the climbing. It couldn't really be heavier than it was before.

Together, they tiptoed into the clearing and looked around. They were very high up the slope now. Mist had rolled down from the mountain peaks and it hung over the grass like a magic spell. On the far side next to a rocky outcrop sat two furry black-and-white shapes, one big and one small.

Clarabel gasped. "Look! There's the little cub with his mother!"

"The cub is so cute!" said Emily, admiringly.

"He's lovely, isn't he!" agreed Jaminta. The panda cub looked up at the sound of her voice, his ears twitching. "I come up here to see him all the time. Now that he's older, he loves to climb and play.

Sometimes his mother leaves him here while she goes to gather more food."

"Have you given him a name?" asked Lulu.

"No, I haven't," said Jaminta. "Maybe we can think of one together."

The mother panda swung around, looking in the direction of their voices. Then she went back to chomping long stems of bamboo again.

"I think they've gotten used to me," added Jaminta. "They don't seem to mind me being here at all."

The mother panda ambled into the forest and the sound of shaking bamboo trees came from her direction.

The princesses watched the little cub bound back and forth underneath the rocky outcrop. Then he climbed up a tree, pulling at the trunk with his little paws. Halfway up, he lost his grip and slid back down, landing on the ground on his furry white bottom.

The princesses giggled.

The cub gave up on the tree trunk and started trying to climb up the rocky outcrop instead. Higher and higher he went, until only his little black legs could be seen below the rock jutting out of the hillside.

The princesses crept closer to watch him, and a sudden weight in her pocket made Jaminta check her rock crystal again. Why did it feel so strange and heavy? She glanced at the other princesses, but they hadn't noticed her worried look.

"I didn't know pandas could climb like that," said Emily.

Just then a noise rang out across the clearing. It was a lovely sound, so high and sweet that for a moment Jaminta thought one of her friends had started singing.

She looked all around the clearing. "What is that sound?"

But the other princesses were staring right at her.

"It's you, Jaminta!" said Lulu. "It's coming from your pocket."

The sound grew louder and even sweeter, rolling around the clearing and into the forest. Feeling like she was dreaming, Jaminta reached into her pocket and pulled out the lump of crystal. It shook as her fingers closed around it, and she knew that it really was this strange, rough gem making the noise. She lifted it up to the light and the sound changed into a sequence of musical notes that rang out like a chiming bell.

There was a silence after the last note died away.

"That was really strange!" cried Emily.

But before Jaminta could speak, a deep cracking noise broke through the still air. A huge chunk of stone fell off the rocky outcrop and crashed to the ground. A cascade of smaller stones followed, and dust rose from the earth below.

The princesses stared in horror at the broken rock.

"Oh no! Where's the cub?" Jaminta cried. "That's where he was climbing!" She started to run toward the rock, her feet flying across the misty grass.

CHAPTER FIVE

Being Lucky

"Wait, Jaminta! What about the cub's mother?" called Emily. "Will she mind you going near her baby?"

But Jaminta kept running, her heart pounding. She'd watched the little panda grow every week since the springtime, and she couldn't stand the thought of him being hurt. Skidding to a halt, she scanned the rocky outcrop. There was a jagged slice right where the stone had broken away.

A thin cry came from the ground. Jaminta knelt down, holding her breath. The panda cub lay among the fallen rubble. The stones seemed to have missed him, except for a rock that lay across his back paw. He wriggled and gave a frightened whimper.

Jaminta reached out and carefully lifted the rock away, setting the little cub free. "There you are. Are you all right now?"

The cub looked up at her, his black eyes solemn.

Amazed at her own daring, Jaminta lifted up the paw that had been trapped and touched it gently. He had soft pads beneath tiny sharp claws, and his fur was so long and soft that it made her want to give him an enormous hug.

"You have to be careful," she told him gently.

The cub yawned, showing rows of little teeth and a pink tongue.

"Is he all right?" asked Clarabel anxiously, as she, Emily, and Lulu reached Jaminta's side.

"He was lucky," Jaminta told them. "One paw was trapped, but there's no sign of injury."

"That's what we should call him — Lucky!" said Emily. "It really suits him!"

The little panda snuffled at Emily's shoes, as if to show that he liked her idea. "Lucky!" murmured Jaminta. "That *is* a good name for him."

"Let's move these stones and clear a path for him." Lulu began moving the fallen rocks aside.

Emily and Clarabel started to help her.

Jaminta looked around, suddenly remembering the mother panda. But there was no sign of her in the clearing.

"Maybe the mother didn't see what happened," she said. "She must still be getting bamboo."

Lucky watched the princesses with his big eyes. His white belly looked plump and fluffy. He rolled onto all fours and walked down the grassy path that the girls had cleared for him. Only the tiniest limp gave away that anything had happened to his back paw.

There was a loud rustling at the edge of the clearing, and the large shape of the mother panda became visible through the trees. The princesses backed away quickly as Lucky skipped over to join his mother. She nudged him with her nose and they walked into the bamboo forest together.

Jaminta gave a deep sigh of relief. "He seems just fine now."

Lulu frowned. "He could have been

really hurt, though. Maybe you shouldn't bring that crystal thing up here again. It's not safe."

Jaminta stared at her. "It wasn't the crystal's fault. I'm sure it wasn't."

"But it did make that really loud singing sound," said Emily. "Sometimes loud noises can cause a rockslide."

"Poor little cub! I'm so glad he's all right," added Clarabel.

Jaminta gazed at the rock crystal in the palm of her hand, her mind whirling. How could they blame the crystal for what happened? She was sure it wasn't a bad jewel. But why had it felt so heavy just before it started to sing? What if they were right and the crystal really had made the rock shatter?

"We're not saying you did it on purpose, Jaminta," said Clarabel. "Please don't be mad."

Jaminta tried to smile. The rock crystal felt light again as she put it back in her pocket.

"I've never heard of a gem making a sound before," said Lulu. "How did you get it to do that?"

"I didn't!" replied Jaminta. "I haven't been able to change its shape at all yet."

"It was such a beautiful song," said Clarabel. "Maybe it means something."

"Maybe," said Jaminta with a frown. "I just wish I knew what it was."

"Come on! Let's go back," said Emily. "It'll be time for the banquet soon."

The mist started to fade as the girls made their way through the forest. They came out of the trees and headed toward the wooden bridge that spanned the river.

"Lucky is so adorable," sighed Clarabel. "I wish we had pandas in my kingdom."

Emily nodded. "He has such lovely little paws!"

They climbed onto the wooden bridge, and Jaminta heard a noise behind them. She looked back, wondering what it was, and glimpsed a flash of red material disappearing between the trees.

CHAPTER SIX

Spotting a Ninja

When they returned, the princesses found that the banquet was almost ready. Sizzling noises came from the kitchen, along with wonderful cooking smells.

The lump of crystal still felt light inside Jaminta's pocket. She clutched it anxiously. Maybe she should take it to the Master Gem Maker and tell him what had happened in the forest. But the sound of the dinner gong stopped her. There was no time to see him now. The banquet was about to begin.

The princesses rushed upstairs to brush their hair and straighten their tiaras. Emily wore her favorite tiara, which had beautiful gold leaves woven together. Clarabel's tiara was made from a delicate wiry gold decorated with sapphires, and Lulu's was a stunning golden crown. Jaminta checked her own tiara in a nearby mirror. It was shaped into three flowers with white crystals glowing on each petal. It was the only tiara she owned that had crystal decorations, and it sparkled like the first snow on the mountains.

The dinner gong sounded again and the girls hurried to the Fan Room to collect the fans they'd chosen earlier.

"We'd better not flick the fans at the banquet," said Clarabel.

"I'll try to remember not to!" Lulu's eyes gleamed teasingly.

Smoothing her green silk dress, Jaminta led the princesses back downstairs to join the crowd of kings and queens in the banquet hall. She blinked as she walked into the room. She'd never seen the hall look so amazing. Masses of gold streamers and round red lanterns hung from the ceiling. The princesses gazed at all the delicious food on the tables.

Jaminta pulled out a chair to sit down and stepped on something hard. She gasped. *Was that somebody's foot?*

"I'm so sorry! I didn't know you were there," she said, looking up to find a tall man with a crooked mouth glaring down at her.

She shivered. He looked so angry that she wondered what he was going to say. But he just turned away, pulling his red cloak around his shoulders. As he marched off, Jaminta suddenly remembered where she'd seen him before. That morning, he had bumped into Ally and knocked over Emily's suitcase. Ally had given him a really strange look and she had wondered why.

"Are you all right?" Clarabel waved her fan next to Jaminta's flushed face.

Jaminta managed a smile. "I'm fine. But I don't think proper princesses are supposed to tread on their guest's toes!"

Emily rushed toward them, nearly knocking a chair over in her hurry. "That's him! That man you just spoke to, Jaminta. He's the one whose voice I recognized. I remember him now!"

"You mean the man who wants to go digging on the mountainside? Are you sure it's him?" said Lulu, looking over Emily's shoulder.

"Completely!" Emily nodded her head knowingly. "He lives in Middingland, where I come from, but he doesn't come to our palace very often." She motioned them toward her, and when their heads were close together, she whispered, "His name is Earl Scrant."

The princesses all looked at the scowling Earl Scrant, who was now standing on the other side of the room. He was wearing shiny black shoes just like the ones they'd seen from underneath the table.

"We'll have to keep an eye on him," said Lulu firmly. "I don't know what he's digging for, but there's something sketchy about him."

The other princesses nodded.

"What are you all whispering about?" Emily's little sister, Princess Lottie, bounced over to them, her bright eyes inquisitive.

"Nothing! Go back to Mom! The banquet's about to start," said Emily.

Lottie pouted. "I know you're talking about something secret and I want to know what it is!"

"Look! Mom's calling you!" said Emily, hurrying her sister away.

The banquet sped by in a jumble of eating, drinking, and talking. The princesses were glad to get away at the end, despite the extra helping of chocolate ice cream they were given. By the time they left the hall, the sun had set and stars had begun to appear in the dark sky.

"That earl with the black shoes has a room just down the hallway from mine," said Lulu. "Let's go and hide nearby so we can see what he does after dinner."

"Great idea!" said Emily. "I want to know what he's doing. I don't trust him one little bit."

They climbed the first set of stairs and walked down the hallway. As they went around a corner, Jaminta caught sight of someone slipping into the shadows behind them.

She flicked her fan open and whispered behind it, "There's someone spying on us! Over there!"

The girls froze.

"What should we do? Should we run away?" muttered Clarabel behind her fan.

"No! Let's pretend we haven't seen them," said Lulu. "Just keep walking."

The princesses climbed up the next staircase. As they reached the top, a shadowy figure moved through the darkness behind them for a second time.

Jaminta felt a tingle run down her spine. She recognized that ninja move. Ally had taught it to them a few months ago, when they were together at Mistberg

Castle. She bit her lip. There was definitely someone sneaking after them, someone who didn't want to be seen.

Glancing back nervously, the princesses scurried down the corridor. Halfway along, Jaminta ducked behind a large dragon statue, making sure she was well hidden by its wooden body. She looked at the others and put a finger to her lips. They nodded quickly and continued walking.

Jaminta crouched down, waiting, her heart thumping.

The shadow flitted closer. It paused for a moment by an open doorway. Then it moved a little closer.

Jaminta held her breath as she watched the shadow edging toward her. What if the ninja had already seen her? For a moment she wished she hadn't hidden here without her friends. But it was

too late now. Feeling shaky inside, she jumped out from behind the dragon statue.

"Stop right now!" she called out, trying to sound brave.

The shadow shrieked and almost fell against the statue.

Jaminta grabbed the shadow's arm to hold it steady.

"Oh, thank you!" said a muffled voice.

Jaminta felt a shock run through her. "Ally? Is that you?" she asked.

The shadow unwound a dark scarf from around her chin. "Yes, it's me!" Ally said, more clearly this time. "Goodness, Jaminta! You made me jump!"

"But, Ally?" Jaminta stared at her. "I don't understand. What's going on? Why are you following us around in the dark?"

CHAPTER SEVEN

The
Ten-Year
Secret

The other princesses raced up to them.

"Ally! What are you doing?" asked Emily, astonished. "You told me you were fixing the bow on my ball gown this evening!"

"You were sneaking after us!" said Lulu, her lionlike eyes flashing.

"No! Not at all!" exclaimed Ally, taking off a black woolen hat and letting her ponytail swing free. "I'm sorry, Your Majesties. I can see why you thought I was following you, but that's not what I was doing at all."

"But you're wearing dark clothes for camouflage," Jaminta pointed out. "And using the ninja moves that you taught us."

"Yes," laughed Ally. "Although I'm obviously not as good as I used to be, because you spotted me easily. You girls are better at the moves than I am." She sighed a little.

The princesses stared at her, a million questions flying through their heads.

"Ally?" asked Emily, at last. "Is there something secret going on?"

Ally looked serious. "We'd better go somewhere more private, where we can talk."

"My room's the closest," said Jaminta.

They hurried into Jaminta's room. Emily, Clarabel, and Lulu settled down on the plump green sofa, while Jaminta lay across the four-poster bed. They looked expectantly at Ally.

"So why *were* you being a ninja?" asked Jaminta.

"All right, I'll tell you," said Ally. "Ten years ago, when I was working as an undercover agent, I was given a very important case. I was asked to find the missing Onica Heart Crystals and catch the thief who stole them."

"Heart Crystals? Were they really famous?" asked Clarabel.

"The Onica Heart Crystals were the most precious jewels in the whole kingdom," explained Jaminta. "There were four of them, each one in the shape of a heart. They were clear, just like diamonds, but had a flickering flame right in the middle. Grandfather told me that he used to keep them in a glass case

in the banquet hall. Then one morning they were gone."

"They were beautiful jewels," Ally agreed. "And really powerful, too. They were supposed to show a person's true nature and whether they were good or evil."

"I've never heard of a jewel that could do that before!" said Emily.

"What happened after they were stolen?" asked Lulu.

"I investigated the robbery for months and months. I followed the trail across the ocean to the kingdom of Middingland." Ally's eyes flicked to Emily, the Middingland princess. "I was there to spy on someone suspicious. But I never managed to find the jewels, and finally I was told to give up. I was working as a maid in Middingland Palace at the time, and I liked it so much that I stayed there."

Emily's mouth dropped open. "Do you mean you were an undercover agent when you became our maid? Being a maid was part of your disguise?"

"It was only a disguise at first." Ally smiled at her. "That was ten years ago. But I could never quite forget the Onica Heart Crystals. They were such special jewels."

A scuffling sound on the roof made them all jump.

Lulu dashed out onto the dark balcony and came back a few seconds later. "It's all right," she panted. "It's only an owl."

"I still don't understand why you were sneaking down the hallway," said Clarabel.

"I always wondered whether the stolen Heart Crystals were actually still here in the kingdom of Onica. Maybe the robber hid them somewhere nearby because he knew we suspected him," explained Ally. "When I saw the man I spied on ten years ago, I couldn't help following him."

"You must be talking about someone from Middingland!" cried Emily.

"Who is it, Ally? You have to tell us!" asked Lulu.

"I don't think I should," said Ally. "I don't want to get you into trouble."

Jaminta frowned for a moment, then her eyes widened. Ally had looked at someone very suspiciously that morning. Jaminta remembered the mysterious look she'd had in her eyes.

Ally got up. "Now I must get back to mending the bow on that ball gown. After that I'll bring you all some mugs of hot chocolate."

As Ally disappeared from the room, Emily turned to the others. "I can't believe Ally kept her secret all this time about why she came to Middingland!"

"I wonder if she's right and the jewels are hidden somewhere nearby," said Lulu excitedly.

"But if they're hidden here, wouldn't someone have discovered them by now?" said Clarabel.

"The jewels *are* hidden here! Don't you see!" Jaminta leapt up, her brown eyes shining. "Ten years ago, Ally went to Middingland to investigate the thief. Emily, you said that Earl Scrant lives in Middingland! And when we hid under that table, we heard him say he wants to dig up something from the mountainside. He must be digging up the stolen Heart Crystals!"

CHAPTER EIGHT

The Magical River

Emily, Clarabel, and Lulu looked at one another, their eyes widening.

"I hadn't thought of that!" said Emily. "I think you're right, Jaminta. Earl Scrant must have stolen the jewels and then buried them on the mountainside in a hurry because he knew he might be caught."

"But what should we do about it?" said Clarabel. "Would your grandfather really believe all this, Jaminta?"

Jaminta shook her head. "We don't have any real proof. We can only tell him what we heard while we were hidden under a table."

"Then we have to make sure we're there when Earl Scrant digs up the Heart Crystals," said Lulu. "If he's caught carrying them, everyone will know he was the thief."

"We can use our ninja moves to follow him," said Emily.

"He won't go up the mountain in the dark, so we can start tomorrow morning, right after we take my rock crystal to the river," added Jaminta.

Lulu and Emily exchanged glances.

"I think we should just concentrate on following Earl Scrant and forget about your crystal," said Lulu.

Emily nodded. "We don't want to miss our chance to find out where the earl will be digging."

"But I have to take the crystal to the river at sunrise. The Master Gem Maker told me to!" cried Jaminta.

Lulu tapped her foot impatiently on the floor. "But this mystery with the earl and the Heart Crystals is *way* more exciting! Anyway, we might get to see Lucky the panda cub again while we're up the mountain!"

"I hope we do!" cried Emily. "He's so adorable! Maybe this time we could pick him some bamboo to eat."

"You shouldn't get too close to Lucky," said Jaminta. "He doesn't know you very well, so he might get scared."

"Oh, don't worry!" said Lulu. "We're Rescue Princesses! I think we know how to take care of animals by now."

Jaminta frowned. She wasn't sure she wanted the other girls getting too close to her cub. After all, she was the one who'd been watching him ever since he was a newborn panda. She was the one who knew him the best.

"I know!" said Clarabel. "Maybe Jaminta and I could go to the river at sunrise, while you two keep an eye on Earl Scrant and find out what he's up to."

"That's a good idea!" said Emily. "That way you can still finish making your new crystal, Jaminta."

Jaminta smiled weakly. She couldn't help wishing she could be at the river *and* up on the mountain with her panda cub at the same time. "All right," she said. "After we finish making the jewel, we'll come to find you as quickly as we can."

Jaminta watched her grandfather's fireworks from her balcony that night. Huge bursts of red and gold blossomed up into the dark sky and twinkled as they fell. After they had ended, she climbed into bed and shut her eyes.

Her mind was buzzing with thoughts. Would the river really change the rock crystal? And would Earl Scrant discover where he'd buried the Heart Crystals all those years ago? She turned over, rubbed her eyes, and fell asleep thinking about Lucky.

She woke the other princesses early the next morning, while it was still dark outside. They sneaked downstairs together, only to find Earl Scrant standing in the hallway as if he was waiting for someone. He raised his eyebrows when he saw them and marched away, frowning.

"Do you think he knows that we figured out he stole the Heart Crystals?" whispered Clarabel.

"I don't know," said Emily. "But he won't see us following him if we use our best ninja moves."

"We'd better go down to the river now, Clarabel. It's nearly sunrise," said Jaminta awkwardly, wishing they were all going together.

"Good luck with your rock crystal," said Emily.

"Thanks." Jaminta bit her lip. "And please be careful about getting close to Lucky. He gets scared really easily."

"Don't worry!" said Lulu firmly. "We know what to do. Come on, Emily!"

The princesses walked out of the palace door and hurried across the garden. Lulu and Emily stopped halfway along the path and waved good-bye to the others. Then they hid behind a large statue of a soldier.

Jaminta and Clarabel raced on, out the

back gate and down the hill, their hair flying out behind them. The sun hadn't risen yet, but the sky was turning from gray to pale yellow. The river lay at the bottom of the valley like a long, glittering ribbon.

"I can see why it's called the Silver River," said Clarabel. "It's so beautiful."

Slowing down, they slipped off their shoes and walked right to the edge of the riverbank, where ducks dabbled in the clear water. Schools of tiny blue fish darted to and fro under the surface. The girls bent over to look at them, making two princess reflections in the water.

"I wish we were all together." Jaminta sighed. "Do you think Lulu still believes that my crystal is dangerous because of the rockslide yesterday?"

"Maybe, but I'm sure she'll change her mind when she sees its new shape," said

Clarabel. "It's really exciting. I've never seen a jewel changed by magic before."

"I really hope it works!" Jaminta waded into the shallows, holding the lump of crystal in one hand. Carefully, she lowered the gem into the water until it lay still on the sandy riverbed. Then she climbed back out and sat on the bank.

"How long will it take?" asked Clarabel.

Jaminta stared into the swirling river. "I don't know. The Master Gem Maker didn't say."

But as they watched, the crystal seemed to grow. Its sides quivered and moved, almost as if it was alive. Then, finally, it settled into a new shape. It wasn't just a lump of whitish rock anymore. Now it was the most beautiful thing they had ever seen, lying sparkling beneath the water.

CHAPTER NINE

The Star Crystal

The two princesses stared at the jewel.

"It's a star!" cried Jaminta.

"Wow, that's amazing!" said Clarabel.

The gem glowed, filling the water with light. Then the brightness faded.

Jaminta waded back in and lifted out the Star Crystal just as the sun rose over the tops of the mountains. She held it up to the sun's first rays and caught her breath. The jewel was now as clear and sparkling as a diamond, and right in the center there was a beautiful flickering fire.

"Is there supposed to be a flame inside it?" said Clarabel, looking alarmed.

"Yes! That's exactly how the Heart Crystals look in all the old pictures." Jaminta turned the Star Crystal over in her hand. Grandfather was going to be so happy with his present. "I wonder if it still makes a singing sound, like it did before," she added thoughtfully.

"You're not taking it up the mountain, are you?" Clarabel gasped. "What if something bad happens?"

"It won't," Jaminta said calmly. "I believe in this jewel. The power inside it is good."

Clarabel looked doubtfully at the Star Crystal, which shone in the growing sunshine.

Just then, a huge black-and-white shape

came out of the bamboo forest on the other side of the river. The mother panda lumbered down the slope and stopped for a moment, pointing her nose toward the two princesses. Then she took a few more strides down to the water and bent her head to drink.

"I've never seen her come right down to the river before," said Jaminta.

"Where's Lucky?" wondered Clarabel, peering hopefully at the forest.

The panda cub sprang out of the trees and ran across the grass toward his mother. He drank from the river for a second, then sat back on his bottom and scratched his furry white stomach with one paw. A bumblebee flew past his nose and he half stood up to swipe at it, but fell over backward instead. His little legs waved wildly in the air.

Jaminta and Clarabel giggled.

"I wish we could stay and watch him all day. He's so cute." Clarabel sighed.

Jaminta put her new Star Crystal into her pocket. "We should probably find the others, though —" she began, but she broke off when her emerald ring lit up brightly. Clarabel's sapphire ring started to glow as well, and a faint voice came through.

"Jaminta? Clarabel? It's Emily! Can you hear me?" Emily's voice sounded worried.

"We can hear you," said Jaminta. "What is it?"

"The earl and his servant are heading your way. Try to follow them," said Emily. "We had to stay away from them because they spotted us and —" Emily's voice crackled and broke off.

Jaminta pressed the emerald on her ring, but the light had vanished.

"Look, Jaminta! Here's the earl," hissed Clarabel.

Two figures came striding out of the back gate and down the hill toward them. The girls pretended to be looking for fish in the river. The man in front was tall and thin, with a crooked mouth and a red cloak that swirled behind him. It was definitely Earl Scrant.

"The servant's got a shovel," muttered Clarabel. "They must be planning to dig for the Heart Crystals right now."

Jaminta tried to glance at them quickly so that they didn't see her looking. She saw the earl's swirling red cloak out of the corner of her eye and it reminded her of something. She'd seen a glimpse of that red cloak before, by the bridge yesterday after they'd visited the pandas.

Earl Scrant climbed onto the curved

bridge and stopped to glare at the two princesses.

"Hey, look, Clarabel!" Jaminta pointed at the water and spoke loudly, her heart thumping. "I just saw some fish."

Both girls leaned over the water, pretending to look.

"Come on, Drudger! Get a move on!" snapped the earl.

The other man followed the earl across the bridge, carrying the shovel balanced over one shoulder. As they reached the other side, the mother panda walked back into the forest, leaving the cub still playing on the riverbank.

Jaminta and Clarabel tiptoed forward. They crept across the bridge, being careful not to make a sound. The two men stopped next to the trees and unfolded a large map.

The princesses edged closer, listening.

"We'll turn right after the rope bridge," said the earl. "Then I'll look for more landmarks."

Jaminta crept a little closer, but her shoe caught on a twig and it broke beneath her foot with an enormous *crack*.

The earl swung around, his eyes bulging. "You silly princesses! How dare you follow me?"

The other man scowled. "That's four of them. If you count the ones we saw in the garden, hiding behind that statue."

The earl ground his teeth. "Stay away from me or I'll make you regret it!"

"We were just leaving." Jaminta went pale. "We won't disturb you." She and Clarabel started backing away, their hearts thumping.

But the earl wasn't paying attention. He had caught sight of the panda cub scampering by the river. He strode over to

Lucky and snatched up the little cub with one gloved hand.

"I know what will stop your meddling," he snapped. "See this pathetic creature that you were cooing over when you crossed the bridge yesterday? Well, if you follow me or if you tell anyone at the palace where I've gone, then you'll never, ever see him again!"

Jaminta's heart turned cold. He was threatening poor Lucky!

The earl's face twisted into a horrible smile. "Do you understand? If you tell or if you follow me, something bad will happen to this animal." He tucked the cub under one arm. "And there are some very steep drops on the mountainside, if you know what I mean." Chuckling to himself, the earl marched into the bamboo forest, with his servant behind him.

Clarabel turned to Jaminta, tears in her

eyes. "What are we going to do? He's taken Lucky and it's all our fault."

Lulu and Emily came sprinting across the wooden bridge.

"What happened?" Lulu panted. "We saw Earl Scrant talking to you. What did he say?"

Jaminta brushed tears from her eyes. "He picked up Lucky and took him away. He said if we followed him, we'd never see Lucky again."

"Oh no!" Emily put her hand over her mouth.

"But we can't leave Lucky with him. He's a dangerous man," cried Clarabel.

Lulu frowned furiously. "I brought some rope in this backpack. Maybe we can capture the earl and tie him up."

"No, he's too big. We'd never be able to do that. We'll have to think of something else." Jaminta gazed up at the mountain, a feeling of calm settling over her. Suddenly, she knew exactly what she had to do. "I know how we can get Lucky back. All we have to do is offer Earl Scrant something he really wants in exchange."

"What do you mean?" asked Emily.

Jaminta drew her hand from her pocket and showed them the beautiful star-shaped jewel. "We give him this. We give him the Star Crystal."

"But, Jaminta!" cried Clarabel. "It's your new jewel. You wanted to give it to your grandfather for his birthday."

Jaminta sighed. "I know. But keeping Lucky safe is more important than anything else in the world!"

CHAPTER TEN

Finding Lucky

"Did your lump of crystal really change into that?" Emily's eyes widened.

Jaminta nodded. "When the earl sees it, I know he'll want it."

"But are you sure it's safe to take your jewel up there?" asked Lulu. "You know what happened last time."

"I'm totally sure," said Jaminta firmly.

"Quick! Or we'll never find Lucky," urged Clarabel.

The four princesses flung themselves into the forest. Jaminta took the lead, stopping to listen now and then, checking the direction of the men crashing through the bamboo trees up ahead. She leaped over a pile of stones and ran on. It was hard trying to be fast and quiet at the same time, but they had to make sure the earl didn't hear them until the very last second.

They stopped at the edge of the rocky ravine.

"This is where we crossed the valley yesterday," said Lulu. "But where's the rope bridge?"

Jaminta pointed down into the ravine, her cheeks flushing angrily. The rope bridge dangled down against the rocky cliff. "It's broken. Earl Scrant must have crossed over and then cut through the rope on the other side."

"What are we going to do?" said Clarabel. "We can't climb all the way down there. It's way too steep."

Jaminta bit her lip. "We have to try something. We have to get to Lucky."

Lulu took off her backpack, reached inside it, and pulled out a long coil of rope. "I'll climb over. Then I can tie one end of this rope to a tree and throw the other end across to you."

The princesses looked across the ravine. The biggest tree on the other side had sturdy branches, strong enough to swing from.

"Will you be able to do it?" Emily looked down at the steep cliff.

Lulu grinned. "Of course! I love climbing!"

She clambered carefully down the rock face, finding handholds and footholds in the rough cliff. Little by little, she lowered herself down.

"You're doing great!" Jaminta called softly as Lulu reached the bottom and began climbing up the other side.

At the top, Lulu tied the rope firmly to a tree and threw the other end across to them.

Jaminta caught it. "Who wants to go first?"

Clarabel's face turned pale. "I can't! It's too far."

"Don't worry. We'll help you." Jaminta put the rope into her hand. "Ready?"

Jaminta and Emily stood behind Clarabel. With a huge push, they swung her across the ravine to Lulu, who caught her safely on the other side. Clarabel hugged Lulu in relief and waved to the others.

Emily swung across next. Then Jaminta stood alone on the edge of the cliff. She took the rope, trying not to look down. There was no one left to push her. She would have to jump hard enough to swing herself all the way across. She lifted her chin. Lucky was probably really scared by now. She would do it for him.

She jumped. The ravine opened out below her, a steep drop filled with jagged rocks. She swung closer to the other side, and just as she wondered if she would make it, three pairs of arms grabbed her.

"Wow!" she gasped, her feet thudding on the ground. "That was pretty scary."

"Right, let's keep going," said Lulu. "We don't want to lose track of the earl."

They hurried on, slipping in and out of the trees, and at last they heard the men moving up ahead. The earl sounded even grumpier than before.

"Hurry up, Drudger!" he snapped. "I want to dig up my jewels and then escape from Onica as fast as possible. But *you* are slowing me down!"

"The shovel is heavy, Your Grace," came the panted reply.

"Shovel! Just be thankful you're not carrying this wretched, squirming animal," said the earl. "If it wriggles again, I'll drop it off the mountain. I'd drop it right now if I could be sure that those frilly princesses aren't following us. But they're tricky! They may have found another way around that ravine."

"But, My Lord? Do you know the right way back to the palace now that you've cut the rope bridge?"

There was a pause.

"I brought you here to dig, Drudger, not to think. I can figure out the way back myself." The earl coughed uneasily. "This is the right place. I'm sure I buried my lovely Heart Crystals here. Start digging at once!"

The princesses crept forward and peered through the bamboo trees into the clearing. The earl still held Lucky carelessly under one arm. The little cub twisted anxiously and let out a tiny whimper. Jaminta longed to hug him and make him feel better.

"I wish we could tie up that nasty earl," hissed Lulu.

"Isn't this where we came before? When we first saw Lucky and that rockslide happened?" whispered Clarabel.

Jaminta glanced around the clearing and nodded. The skin on the back of her neck tingled. Something important was about to happen here. Somehow, she just knew it was.

"Do you really think you should take the crystal in there?" said Emily.

Jaminta drew the Star Crystal from

her pocket. Inside its diamond-clear shape, the flame burned brightly. "This is the only thing I've got that the earl will want in exchange for Lucky." She took a deep breath. "Ready, everyone?"

The others nodded. Together, they stepped out of their hiding place into full view.

"You again!" yelled the earl. "This time you will be sorry —"

But Jaminta interrupted him. "Stop! We've come to ask for the panda cub in exchange for this crystal." She held the Star Crystal out for him to see.

The earl's eyebrows rose. "What? Where did you get that from?"

"Never mind where we got it!" said Jaminta, her voice trembling. "It's a Star Crystal and you can have it if you hand over the cub right now."

The earl strode toward her and snatched the Star Crystal out of her hand, dropping Lucky on the ground without a second thought.

Jaminta ran to Lucky, gathering the little cub into her arms and feeling his soft black-and-white fur against her cheek. "Lucky!" she whispered. "I'm so glad you're safe!"

Lucky squeaked happily and snuffled into her ear.

The earl's face broke into a twisted smile of delight as he gazed at the sparkling Star Crystal. "This will truly make me rich!" He turned to his servant. "Now, Drudger! Tie up these nosy princesses!"

But the other man wasn't listening. He dropped his shovel and looked around with wide eyes. A sound began to rise above the bamboo trees, clear and sweet. The Star Crystal had started to sing.

Sister Jewels

Jaminta backed away, holding Lucky tightly in her arms. The other princesses edged backward, too.

"What's going on?" moaned the earl.

The song became higher and more haunting, weaving around them like the wind. The earl dropped the Star Crystal and put his hands over his ears. The rocky outcrop behind the men began to shudder. The earth trembled. An enormous splinter of stone broke off and shattered on the ground below.

"The mountain's falling down!" cried the earl.

The two men ran away, stumbling over rocks and crashing through trees as they fled back down Cloud Mountain.

The princesses stood their ground. Jaminta held on to Lucky even tighter, while he buried his head in her shoulder.

The Star Crystal sang a final, piercing note, which made the earth rumble and opened up a gaping hole in the ground. Then the song faded away to nothing and the mountainside stopped shaking. One last swirl of dust rose from the fallen stones and floated away.

Jaminta breathed deeply in the sudden silence. She looked around, stroking

Lucky's soft fur. She was so glad that he was safe and no one had been hurt.

"That was weird," said Emily. "I felt like the Star Crystal wanted something. Like it was talking."

Clarabel nodded. "I thought that, too."

Lulu darted forward to look inside the hollow that had opened in the ground. "Come and see this! There's something in here." She climbed down into the hole and picked up a small brown sack lying at the bottom.

The girls gathered around as Lulu undid the string at the top and turned the sack upside down. Four beautiful heart-shaped crystals tumbled out onto the grass. Each one was sparkling and transparent, but with a tiny flame in the center.

Clarabel picked one up. The Heart Crystal sparkled between her fingers.

"The Onica Heart Crystals!" Jaminta gasped. "Grandfather will be so happy that they've been found!"

"So will Ally!" said Emily. "I can't wait to tell her!"

"You were right, your crystal wasn't a bad jewel at all," said Lulu. "We should have believed you, Jaminta."

Jaminta smiled back at them. "I knew it couldn't be bad. It must have been trying to find the Heart Crystals all along. It was singing to set them free." She gave Lucky a squeeze and patted his furry head.

Emily picked up the Star Crystal from where the earl had dropped it and laid it next to the Heart Crystals. The five gems glowed together for a second. "Look! They're like sister jewels."

Behind them came a loud rustling, and the mother panda lumbered into the clearing. Lucky let out a soft squeak and licked Jaminta's hand.

"There you go, little Lucky." Jaminta set him gently down onto the ground.

"He's safe now that the earl has run away," said Emily.

Lucky ran over to his mother, who nuzzled him lovingly.

Jaminta smiled as she watched them amble away across the grass. Lucky turned to look at her one more time before he followed his mother into the forest.

Jaminta picked up the jewels and gave one Heart Crystal to each of her friends.

"Let's go back to the palace and show these jewels to my grandfather," she said. "It will be a perfect birthday present for him!"

CHAPTER TWELVE

The Heart Crystals Come Home

The princesses hurried through the palace gate. It had taken them a long time to find a way back that avoided the rocky ravine with its broken rope bridge. A loud cheer rose as they walked into the garden. The girls looked at one another in surprise, but the crowd of people standing on the grass was all facing the other way.

"What's going on?" whispered Clarabel.

Jaminta tried to peer through the mass

of people, but she could only see arms and legs.

"Your grandfather's standing next to his birthday cake," called Lulu, who had climbed halfway up the soldier statue. "I think we're going to sing 'Happy Birthday' to him next."

Jaminta's mom noticed the girls and frowned at the sight of their muddy dresses. "Princesses! Where have you been? Jaminta, you're absolutely covered in dirt and leaves. Go upstairs and change at once!"

"But, Mom! We found something really amazing," said Jaminta, trying to show her the Heart Crystal. "And I don't want to miss Grandfather's party."

"Jaminta! You can't stand here with twigs in your hair!" said the queen of Onica sternly.

Jaminta swept a hand over her dark hair and pulled out a clump of twigs. She made a face and turned toward the palace.

"Is that my lovely granddaughter?" called Emperor Cho from the front. "Come up here, Jaminta!"

Jaminta brushed the leaves off her dress and made her way through the crowd until she stood next to her grandfather. "Happy birthday, Grandfather!" she said, hugging him. "I have a special present to give you!"

Her grandfather's eyes twinkled. "Is it a surprise?"

Jaminta grinned. "I guess it is! You see, I tried to make a beautiful crystal to give to you, and it finally worked." She dropped the Star Crystal into his wrinkled hand. "And then this star jewel helped me find these crystals as well."

She dropped one of the Heart Crystals into his hand, too.

Emperor Cho stared at the magical crystals in silent amazement. Lulu, Emily, and Clarabel came to the front and showed him the other three heart-shaped gems.

"Happy birthday, Grandfather!" said Jaminta softly.

"The stolen crystals!" said the emperor, gazing at the sparkling jewels. "How did you find them after all this time?"

"They were buried on the mountainside," explained Jaminta. "The thief hid them there, planning to dig them up later."

"But who hid them?" The emperor looked all around, as if he was expecting the thief to jump out of the crowd.

"It was Earl Scrant, Your Majesty!" said Emily, with a curtsy. "We saw him trying to dig up the jewels today."

"Really? Earl Scrant?" echoed the emperor in astonishment.

The kings and queens muttered to one another and shook their heads.

"Look! There he is!" someone called, and the crowd turned to look at a tall, thin figure that was hurrying toward the palace gates with a suitcase.

"Guards! Arrest him!" called Emperor Cho.

Earl Scrant saw the guards chasing him and began to run. He dropped his suitcase, which sprang open. Jaminta's tiara fell out onto the walkway. The crowd gasped. The earl was caught by the guards and taken away.

"Well, this *is* a day of big surprises!" said the emperor. "I'm so very proud of you, Jaminta. You discovered something that has been lost for ten years."

The queen sniffed. "I *suppose* you did very well to find them, even though your dresses are very dirty."

Jaminta chewed her lip. "But . . . I nearly gave all these jewels away to save a panda cub."

Her grandfather burst out laughing. "That's because you're a kind-hearted girl. Have I ever told you the true power of these Heart Crystals?"

Jaminta shook her head.

Emperor Cho gave her the heart-shaped jewel back. "Blow on the crystal very gently. You try it, too, girls."

The princesses all blew gently on the Heart Crystals. As their breaths touched the jewels, their transparent surfaces filled with beautiful color. Jaminta's gem turned green, Emily's was red, Clarabel's was blue, and Lulu's was bright yellow. A

murmur of astonishment rippled around the crowd.

"They've turned the same colors as our rings," whispered Jaminta.

"These crystals show the true nature of a person's heart," said the emperor. "I suspect if Earl Scrant blew on one of these gems it would turn black, revealing him for the scoundrel he is. But each of you has a very good heart indeed."

The crowd clapped and cheered.

"I want you to keep this star jewel, Jaminta," the emperor continued, "to remind you of this special day. Having these Heart Crystals back is enough of a birthday present for me."

"Thank you, Grandfather!" said Jaminta.

"Well done, princesses!" whispered Ally, who had come to see the celebrations. "Ten years after they vanished, the Heart

Crystals are finally back where they belong."

Emperor Cho asked his guards to put the Heart Crystals away safely in a display cabinet in the banquet hall. Then they all sang "Happy Birthday" and ate several slices of cake. The twelve-tier birthday cake kept everyone happy, with its layers of chocolate fudge, cherry, ginger, lemon, toffee, and many other flavors. Emily's little sister, Lottie, ate a slice from all twelve tiers and then had to sit very still on a garden chair to settle her aching stomach.

Jaminta linked arms with the others as they went to get glasses of lemonade. "I know we don't agree all the time, but I'll never forget all the things we've done together."

"Me neither," said Lulu.

"The adventures just get better and better," said Clarabel, with a happy sigh.

"Maybe one day we'll find more princesses who'd like to join us," said Emily, skirting around her sister, Lottie, who was now turning cartwheels across the grass.

"I'm sure lots of girls would love to join," agreed Jaminta. "After all, who could say no to a life full of jewels, banquets, and ninja training?"

The Rescue Princesses
are on another daring
animal adventure!

The Snow Jewel

Turn the page for
a sneak peek!

CHAPTER ONE

Sledding at the Castle

Princess Freya sped across the crisp snow in her thick furry boots. Her blond braids bounced on her shoulders and her blue eyes shone brightly.

She ran through the gate at the end of the castle garden and closed it behind her. Then she stopped for a moment to gaze down the hill at the newly made ice rink at the bottom. Fresh snow had fallen in the night and the sunshine was making everything sparkle.

A group of princes raced out of the gray stone castle behind her and began throwing snowballs at one another. Freya swung around to watch them. It was strange seeing her castle so busy and noisy when it was usually so quiet.

Her dad, King Eric, had invited all the royal families from around the world to come and spend the winter holidays here in the kingdom of Northernland. The ice rink had been dug out and smoothed over especially for everyone to skate on. The guests had arrived yesterday, and now the castle was crammed with kings, queens, princes, and princesses.

Freya took a few steps down the hill, thinking about the other princesses. She had been longing to meet some girls her own age for what seemed like forever. She'd seen four princesses slip out the door after breakfast. They had run off laughing together and she had desperately wanted to join them. But where had they gone?

The sound of giggling floated over to her on the frosty air. Freya hurried down the slope and through a cluster of fir trees, trying to see where the noise was coming from. When she reached the other side of the trees, she saw the girls right away.

Four princesses, wearing thick coats, woolen scarves, and gloves, were pulling a wooden sled up the hill. When they reached the top, a girl with wavy black hair sat down on the sled and the others gave her a huge push.

The princess on the sled zoomed away with a shout of delight. Halfway down the hill, she jumped on top of the sled and glided the rest of the way standing on one leg. Freya's eyes widened. She'd

ever seen somebody do such a daring trick before!

The black-haired princess jumped off at the bottom of the slope, and the others ran down to help her pull the sled back up. A princess with red curls noticed Freya and waved.

"Hello!" called the red-haired princess. "Would you like to come and try?"

Freya blushed and ran over. "Thanks! That's really nice of you!"

"It's not really *that* nice!" The princess laughed. "We borrowed this sled from the castle. So it's really yours! I'm Princess Emily, by the way."

"And I'm Lulu," said the black-haired princess. "This is Jaminta." She pointed at a girl with smooth dark hair. "And that's Clarabel." She pointed at a girl with golden hair.

"Hello," said Jaminta and Clarabel, smiling widely.

"I'm Freya," said Freya shyly. "I'm so pleased that you've all come to stay. I've wanted to meet some other princesses for a long time."

"Didn't you come to the Mistberg Grand Ball last year?" asked Lulu, looking at Freya curiously.

Freya shook her head. "My dad likes to stay here at home in Northernland."

"Well, I think it's wonderful here in the snow." Emily smiled at her. "Would you like the next turn on the sled?"

Freya beamed back. "Yes, please!"

The five princesses grabbed the rope and pulled the sled up to the top of the hill. Then Freya got the sled into position and climbed on.

"Try going down backward," cried Lulu, jumping up and down. "It's really fun!"